To Will and Wyatt, my inspiration for everything!
-Mom

To Wells and Barrett with all my love
-Mom

Four Boys Industries, LLC
191 University Blvd #560 Denver, CO 80206

ISBN: 978-0-692-22213-3

Library of Congress Control Number: 201494118

ISBN: 978-0-692-22213-3

Library of Congress Control Number: 201494118

www.switchcrafted.com

FOUR BOYS

Industries, LLC

Switchcrafted™

The Story of the Switch Witches of Halloween

written by

Audrey Kinsman

with

Pam Hatcher

Have you ever wondered why
Witches are part of Halloween?
But the rest of the year,
they are rarely ever seen?

Witches come out on Halloween
because they have magic to do,
They **MUST** gather bags of **CANDY**
from good kids like you.

Witches can cast spells
and make magic as you know,
But they have no spell
to make candy, it just isn't so.

Without candy, the magic world
of Witches will not survive,
As candy creates the power that
keeps the Witch world alive!

Witches do not eat candy,
although some may try.
However, candy is the only fuel
that makes a Witchy broom fly!

Chocolate is the energy
that warms their cold
Witchy homes,

And gummies heat the bathwater for their achy Witchy bones.

Candy is a sweet treat for you and for me, but for any ordinary Witch, it's a necessity!

4

To solve their candy shortage,
Witches have tried trick-or-treating,
But failed to blend in with others that evening.
On Halloween night the magic they do,
Largely depends on little old YOU!

So the Witches make deals
with only good girls and boys,
"If you leave us your candy,
We will Switchcraft it for toys!"

Gathering your treats gives
Witches much work to do,
They have continents to cover -
an ocean or two.

So they nominated the finest
and fastest Witches of all,
Who, like most Witches,
are crafty, sneaky and tall.

These Switch Witches are
picked and ordained with a spell,
They have the power of Switchcraft
and it's your candy they smell!

8

The black clothes they wear
will provide a disguise,
So they can fly down your chimney,
then back out to the skies.

Your Witch is ok with you keeping
a few pieces of loot,
But eat is all up
and she'll leave nary a newt.

Your Switch Witch is nimble and travels quite light,
While her frog and tabby cat sort candy all night.

For those who've been naughty,
or even less than a joy,
Your Switch Witch won't Switchcraft
your candy for a toy!

12

One thing I cannot tell you, you will have to decide on your own,
Is a name for your Switch Witch, and perhaps a spot in your home.

She spends all of October
Watching the good things you do,
She also makes notes
of your bad moments too!

Remember that only good
kids can trade,
So be on your best behavior,
and a Switchcraft will be made.

If you think you have been mostly good
and would like to make a deal,
Write to your Switch Witch stating your appeal.

Remember to describe
the toy you've desired,
And a back up or two in case
that spell's now expired!

The next Halloween as you go trick-or-treating,
Keep the Witches in mind, and their need for winter heating.

Haul in as much candy as you can hold in your tote,
Then leave it out for your Switch Witch, along with your note.

The Witches will all thank you
as they stay warm through the year,
and your Switchcrafted toy will magically appear!

On this spooky and enchanted October day,

The _Martinez_ family invited

their Switch Witch to come for a stay.

They named her _Theodora_ ♡ and from

that day on, she would watch and report on

the family's goings on. Switchcrafting candy

for toys, for all the good girls and boys.